THE DESCENT

THE DESCENT

DRAGON APPROVED™ BOOK SIX

RAMY VANCE

MICHAEL ANDERLE

LMBPN

DISRUPTIVE IMAGINATION®

THE DESCENT TEAM

Thanks to the JIT Readers

Dave Hicks
Kathleen Fettig
Diane L. Smith
John Ashmore
Deb Mader
Kelly O'Donnell
Dorothy Lloyd
Larry Oman

If I've missed anyone, please let me know!

Editor
The Skyhunter Editing Team

Copyright © 2020 by Ramy Vance & Michael Anderle
Cover Art by Jake @ J Caleb Design
http://jcalebdesign.com / jcalebdesign@gmail.com
Cover copyright © LMBPN Publishing
A Michael Anderle Production

LMBPN Publishing
PMB 196, 2540 South Maryland Pkwy
Las Vegas, NV 89109

First US Edition, March 2020
Version 1.02, October 2020
eBook ISBN: 978-1-64202-785-3
Print ISBN: 978-1-64202-786-0

DEDICATION

To Wee Orla... you should be here by now!

—Ramy

To Family, Friends and
Those Who Love
to Read.
May We All Enjoy Grace
to Live the Life We Are
Called.

— Michael

CHAPTER ONE

Alex impatiently tapped her feet while she stood outside, waiting for Team Boundless to meet her. She'd already been waiting for an hour, and patience was not one of her virtues. She'd become very aware of that fact.

Waiting for the team was much better than waiting for the higher-ups to take her seriously. At least the team was going to show up.

When Alex had decided that Boundless was going to go help Roy and Toppinir, she'd thought they would just jump on their dragons and head out. Then Gill had brought Alex back down to reality and explained what they would have to do before they could get moving.

The dragons had just been in an impressive and taxing battle a few hours before. Maintenance had to be the first and foremost priority if the dragons were going to be moving again. The dragons could very easily get hurt if their equipment was not maintained, not to mention, they needed a break.

Alex had jumped at the chance to do anything to help

Chine feel better. She hadn't been aware that he had been in any kind of pain. None of the dragons seemed to have been damaged during the battle, and she had completely forgotten what she'd been told when she was back at the Nest.

Gill once more burst Alex's bubble. It wasn't as simple as just going to change out their dragon's equipment. They would need access to the stables in *this* facility—the facility they weren't supposed to be exploring. The same facility where everyone was on edge and which was filled with patrols.

"I see your point," Alex had said. "You're basically telling me we have no options. We just have to sit around, even though we all agreed that we're going to help Toppinir and Roy. That is what you're saying, right, Gill?"

Gill had taken a deep breath and launched into a lengthy explanation of his plan to get the team out of the facility with their dragons healthy and newly equipped. The plan was long. And complicated. There were moments Alex thought Gill might have snapped under the pressure. But it *was* a plan —that much she could be certain of.

The team had decided to go with Gill's plan, seeing as how they didn't have any other options. That was why Alex was waiting outside, very aware that she wanted to be pacing and even more aware that pacing would just draw more attention to her. Which was not in the plan.

Gill, Brath, Jim, and Jollies exited the facility and rushed over to Alex. Jim and Gill were carrying a couple of video cameras and cords that they packed onto Jim's back. Brath was playing with a set of keys. "What are those for?" Alex asked.

Brath tossed the keys to Alex. "We're going on a little joyride," Brath replied.

Team Boundless rolled down the quarry, driving a yeti ATV. Naturally, the ATV was nearly twice the size of a regular ATV, and as a result, Alex and the others had to come up with a creative way to drive the beast of a machine.

Alex and Gill were given brake and accelerator duty. They were both down at the bottom of the ATV, shoved together tighter than Alex liked. As they worked the two pedals, their hands occasionally brushed.

Gill didn't seem to notice. Alex *tried* not to notice Gill not noticing.

Jim sat on a milk crate in front of the passenger seat, working the clutch. For some reason, yeti ATVs required two yetis to operate them, possibly because they were so large and demanding.

Whenever Brath shouted, "Shifting," Jim would kick down on the clutch so that Jollies, who was zipping around in the ATV, could slam against the gear shifter and move it to the appropriate gear.

Brath was taking care of the steering. He was the oldest of the team members. Alex found this extremely surprising because Brath seemed like the least mature of the group. But as the oldest, he had been the only one who knew how to drive.

The ATV bumped up and down as Brath steered over a large rock. "How did you ever get a chance to drive?" Alex asked from the bottom of the ATV. "Do gnomes even have cars?"

Brath struggled with the wheel as he tried to rein in the beastly ATV. "I mean, they're close enough to human cars," Brath explained. "They're kinda slower and clunkier, kinda like your human's steampunk nonsense. Except ours actually work well. Mostly dwarfish style. You know, similar heights."

"You probably should have taken more driving lessons."

Brath pulled hard to the right, swinging the ATV around the canyon's corner. "I don't see anyone else with anything close to driving experience!" Brath shouted as his face went red. "Anyone who has that is more than welcome to get up here and start steering."

Alex and Gill snickered from the bottom of the ATV as Brath continued to mutter under his breath about how underappreciated he was. "So, why are we doing all of this, Gill?" Brath shouted.

The ATV shuddered as Brath tried to guide it toward the canyon's walls, where the slope was low enough for him to start climbing. "We are doing this as part of a diversion," Gill explained. "We need to get the soldiers out of the facility so we can access the dragons."

Jim, who was staring out the window, jumped as Brath shouted, "Shift! Then speed up!"

Once the team had changed gears, Jim asked, "How does becoming an A/V team help us to get everyone out of the facility?"

The ATV started to climb the canyon. It instantly began losing speed, its wheels churning through the gravel as Alex panicked and hit her pedal, causing the ATV to speed up. Brath shouted, "Clutch," and Jim slammed down on the clutch while Jollies screeched, "Shift!"

They continued on in this way, the ATV a collection of shouting voices: Brath trying to direct what action needed to be fulfilled, Alex trying to stifle her nervous giggles, and Jollies cursing under her breath in Pixie.

As they climbed the mountain, Gill went further into the plan. They were going to draw out the soldiers with a ploy. Over in the canyon, where they had battled the trolls, there was plenty of material to work with.

A second attack by the trolls would light a fire under the

asses of the soldiers at the facility. They wouldn't be able to ignore it. It wasn't as if the soldiers were going to help Roy and Toppinir since the facilities' resources were already low.

Alex thought the idea sounded far-fetched and hard to believe. Why not just start a fire in the facility? When Alex pressed Gill on the details, he merely shrugged and said, "Outside the facility is better. We have more control and a longer window of time to work in."

So, Alex accepted that it was going to be out of her control. The more she thought about it, though, the more she was all right with it. She'd been calling most of the shots since they left on their mission, but she knew her team was capable.

Why not find out their strengths?

After another twenty minutes of fighting with the ATV (and each other), Team Boundless arrived at the bloodstained battlefield. There hadn't been enough time for the trolls and vrosks to start rotting. Still, Alex was taken aback by the scene. When they were fighting, she had been in the frenzy of battle, and she hadn't really thought much about what she had done. There hadn't been time, but now there was.

The canyon was quiet, the only sound a breeze rustling through. This felt like a solemn moment, and Alex tried to take it all in. It was different than in Middang3ard; after the battles in VR, players had cracked jokes, and there had been an air of levity. Nothing like this.

They weren't standing in the middle of a virtual battle-ground. This was a field of death. Vultures were already starting to descend on their oddly winged brethren, lying dead on the floor of the canyon.

Jim whistled. "Man, those dragons can really tear things up."

Alex started heading toward the field to get a better look

at the carnage the dragonriders had left in their wake. "Yeah, that's an understatement," she replied. "Seriously, those beasts are powerful. Extremely powerful."

A thought crossed Alex's mind, and she turned back to face the other dragonriders. "Hey, if dragons are this powerful, what the hell does the Dark One have up his sleeve that's causing so much trouble for the rest of the dragonriders?"

Jollies was flying back and forth, looking at all the bodies. "That's a good question," she answered. "As far as I know, dragons are the be-all and end-all of creatures. The wisest, the strongest...you know, pretty much the top of the line."

"Yeah, back in VR, dragons were mostly end-game. Nothing you took lightly," Alex agreed. "But if you could take down a dragon, you could take down anything. What is this guy using that could take down dragons?"

Gill was already farther down the canyon, walking among the bodies. Jim was with him and they were talking quietly, Gill pointing to places where he wanted Jim to set up a camera.

Brath came up behind Alex and stood next to her. He didn't say anything, but Alex could see that he was watching Gill and Jim closely. She thought it might be jealousy since she'd noticed that Jim and Gill seemed to get along very well. Brath probably felt threatened. Alex leaned over to Brath and nudged him.

Brath looked up at Alex, annoyed. "What?" he growled.

"Jealous much?"

"What? Of what?"

Alex tilted her head in the direction of Gill and Jim. "You know you can go over there and help them."

Brath scoffed loudly and folded his arms. "If Gill wanted my help, he would have asked for it instead of asking Jim."

"Or maybe he just assumed you knew he'd like your help.

You two already know each other. He's probably just trying to help Jim feel like he's part of the team. He hasn't known us as long as we've known each other."

Brath threw his hands in the air as he walked off. "I don't need any advice," he shouted.

Alex noticed that Brath was heading in Gill and Jim's direction. The gnome had gotten the point. Now she was free to wonder about the vast complexities of the universe, especially the part where she was unlucky enough to have a crush on two guys who were becoming fast friends.

The three boys worked on setting up the cameras as Jollies and Alex stayed farther back in the canyon, keeping watch for any troll patrols or other dragonriders. Jollies sat on Alex's shoulder as usual, chattering nearly too fast for Alex to understand.

Sometimes Jollies got like that. It meant she was either excited or nervous, and at the moment, it seemed like too much excitement. She was curious to know how the plan was going to work out. Alex, on the other hand, was trying to keep her pessimism to herself.

Finally, the boys finished placing the cameras. Alex and Jollies came over to check out their work. Altogether, there were ten cameras placed around the circumference of the battlefield. In addition, there were also ten cameras on the ground, facing up at the sky.

Alex pointed at one of the cameras looking skyward. "Okay, so you're going to have to explain exactly what you're doing," she said. "Because it looks like a really weird photography project."

Gill slid up his visor and sat down on a rock as he scrolled through menus, occasionally looking at his dragon anchor. "I'm creating a digital construction," Gill explained. "Basically, a virtual reality simulation, or more like a computer-generated image—the kind that humans use for their movies. The sky acts as the green screen. The bodies are assets."

"You're making a movie?"

"A movie of our trolls' reinforcements. Then I'm going to hack into the security systems at the facility and replace their feed with the one that I made."

Gill pointed to the canyon, and Alex noticed that there were cameras sporadically placed that were used for the facility's security. "Wait," Alex asked. "Why didn't the facility send reinforcements when we were being attacked?"

"Because they're understaffed. Also, the cameras have a delay, which we can use to our advantage. We'll head back after I upload the video. By the time we get back, they should be sending out their reinforcements."

Jim gave Gill a high five and said, "Dude, that's sick. Using their own tech against them."

Brath chimed in, speaking a little too loudly and eagerly. "Yeah, that's amazing, Gill."

All of the riders turned and looked at Brath, surprised by something other than smugness or carefully cultivated disinterest. Brath blushed under their gaze. "I mean, it is," he muttered. "You're always coming up with cool stuff. Just thought you should know."

Gill smiled as if he had known all along about Brath's jealousy over his new friendship with Jim. "Thanks, Brath," he said. "I always appreciate your support."

Brath huffed and puffed loudly as he folded his arms and turned. "You don't have to go making it all weird," he mumbled.

Team Boundless waited while Gill worked on constructing the computer-generated troll horde, which took nearly twenty minutes. The team made conversation during that time, Alex occasionally paying attention when anyone other than Jim spoke. But mostly she zoned out.

Finally, Gill flipped his visor down and stood. "All right. Just sent it through. Let's get out of here and head back."

CHAPTER TWO

Team Boundless made their way back to the military facility. They were still having a hard time working together to operate the ATV, but after some readjusting, they found a better system. Alex was still at the bottom of the ATV, but Gill and Jim had switched places.

Jollies wasn't working the shift anymore; that was Brath's job. Instead, she was a lookout, watching to make sure they didn't come across any of the riders from the facility. Being spotted would be the end of their plan. That was what Gill said, anyway, when Jollies pouted about having her position snagged.

Alex was glad Gill had stepped in and said something before she did. She'd noticed that Jollies could go from excited to sullen in a split second. The pixie's temperament was not something to take lightly.

As they made their way through the canyon, focusing on staying at the top so they could keep an eye on what was going on beneath them, Alex concentrated on ignoring Jim. She had only just got out of this same situation with Gill. There wasn't anything more uncomfortable than being shoved as close as possible to a boy she liked.

Jim being Jim made it a thousand times worse. He wasn't as kind or brooding as Gill (which, Alex admitted, was a very interesting combination). Jim was normal and human.

The ATV bounced upward and Brath shouted, "Brakes!"

Jim leaned forward and pressed down on the brakes as Alex took her hand off the accelerator. The ATV jerked forward as it slowed down, and Brath shifted the gears. "I don't ever want to drive like this again," Jim said, laughing.

The ATV was slowing too much, so Alex lightly pressed down on her pedal. "Yeah, seriously, this is the most stressed out I've ever been in a car," she agreed. "Never would have thought yetis being so huge would annoy me so much."

The ATV jiggled and jerked again, and Brath started shouting out commands again. Alex was only half-listening when she felt Brath's foot kick her shoulder for not pressing the pedal hard enough. "Hey, watch it!" Alex shouted at Brath before turning back to Jim.

Jim laughed as he moved around, trying to get comfortable, which caused him to practically lean against Alex, who held her breath as her heart raced.

Jim reached up and tugged on Brath's pantleg. "Hey, Brath! How long did you live with your parents?" he asked.

Brath warily looked down at Jim for a second. "That's kinda a personal question. Why are you trying to get to know me all of a sudden?" he asked.

"It's just a question. I'm not trying to build a profile on you or anything. Just getting to know the team."

Brath sighed as he turned his attention back to the road. "I moved out when I was six," he said. "And I was a late one. My mom and dad said that Brorn, my sister, moved out when she was three. Psh. I would have too, if I could. Mom and Dad are so annoying."

Alex could hardly wrap her head around what Brath had just said. She couldn't imagine leaving home as a baby. Even now, it wasn't like she had put a lot of thought into moving out. She wasn't planning on living with her folks forever, but there just didn't seem to be a rush to be gone.

That was probably why Alex was so surprised at becoming a dragonrider. In some ways, she had always assumed she was going to be at home. The outside world hadn't seemed to be an adventure she was going to have. Turned out, though, she was dead wrong.

Brath's voice broke over the grinding of gears. "Gill, you gotta pop the clutch!" he shouted. "Pop the damn thing!"

Gill took a moment to respond. "Popping the clutch is the opposite of how you are supposed to change gears. That's why the ATV keeps surging. You have to be restrained, Brath."

Alex wondered if Jim knew how she felt about Gill. Brath obviously did. And so did Jollies. In all honesty, Gill probably knew as well. It was an uncomfortable feeling, as if Alex's emotions were on display for the entire team to see.

It didn't really matter, though, not in the long run. All Alex had to do was keep it from getting in the way of the mission. Even if internally, she felt like she was in a very bad nineties sitcom, that didn't mean she had to act like it. Sure, she was a teenager, but she knew she could behave maturely.

That was when Alex decided she wasn't going to worry about choosing anyone. Nothing was ever that simple. In every book she'd ever read, the hero would work themselves into a frenzy, trying to choose the love of their life.

Things were always messy in love triangles, at least in stories. Alex had never been in a real one before. She'd never had a crush on anyone, even. But she felt like she could manage the situation without it devolving into meme-level stupidity. Whatever happened, happened. It was that simple.

Alex felt like a huge weight had been lifted from her chest, and she breathed easily for the first time since she'd been at the bottom of the ATV with one of the boys she liked. This was doable. Besides, there was the whole Dark One and end-of-the-world thing to focus on.

Jollies squealed and broke into Alex's train of thought. The pixie was zooming back and forth in the ATV's cockpit. "There they are, there they are!" she chirped, pointing toward the canyon's edge. "We gotta check it out."

Barth gave Jollies a confused look. "How do you know they're down there?" he asked. "They'd be down over the ridge."

Jollies flashed bright red for a second before mellowing out. "It's kinda like a sixth sense," she explained. "I can pick up on people's emotions, especially strong ones. When a lot of people are feeling similar things, it's like a light bulb going on in my head."

Jollies pointed toward the canyon and said, "There's a lot of anxiety making its way through the canyon. They're heading for the battlefield."

Gill stared out his window, trying to get a glance at what might be happening down in the canyon. When he couldn't see anything, he pulled up his HUD visor and looked through the cameras he had placed there. "They've still got a ways to go."

Alex shouted from the bottom of the ATV, "How long, do you think?"

"Another twenty minutes to get there. Ten to figure out what's going on. Then another twenty for them to get back."

"Sweet, so we've got like an hour?"

"*Not* sweet. It's going to take us some time to get the dragons ready. An hour is pushing it. You've never done maintenance before, have you? It's time-consuming."

Alex pushed down hard on the accelerator. "Then we're going to need as much time as we can get!"

The ATV sped along the canyon, the team finally starting to get a good flow among themselves of switching gears and maintaining speed. Everyone was silent, worrying about their time constraints.

Alex wasn't worried, though. She was trying to figure out ways they could reduce wasted time. "Hey, Gill!" she shouted. "Can you hack into their equipment system?"

Gill pulled up his visor again and started scrolling. "Of course. What do you need to know?"

"Start prepping their dragon stables. Link everyone up so they can start going through their options. That way, we won't be sitting around trying to figure out what equipment we want to use. We can just take care of the dragons and get the hell out."

Gill flashed Alex a thumbs-up and got to work. It wasn't long before he had patched everyone into the stable's system. Now the team was quiet because they were going over their options, which was a better use of their time than worrying.

Alex kept a constant speed so the rest of the team didn't have to stress about their roles. Brath was the only one who had to focus, but as he had said, he didn't need to look at the equipment options. Furi hated just about everything and only used fire anyway.

Alex still wasn't sure how far Chine's telepathy stretched, but she figured it wouldn't hurt to try. She reached out to Chine, thinking, *Hey, if you can hear me, could you meet us outside? We kinda did something stupid and need to get going as soon as possible.*

Much to Alex's surprise, Chine's voice came through loud and clear. *Oh, you did? Why am I not surprised to hear that?*

Well, they left us alone for so long. What was I supposed to do?

I take it we will be leaving soon?

Yeah. As soon as we can.

Chine laughed softly and replied, *Good. None of us dragons quite likes it here. It lacks the splendor of the Nest. We'll meet you outside.*

It took about fifteen minutes for the team to finally arrive back at the facility. They took the ATV around to the back, just in case there were still other riders around. Alex knew that if even one person saw them, it was over.

Team Boundless snuck around the back of the facility while she telepathically let Chine know where they were heading. Occasionally, she peeked through the facility's windows to see if anyone had stayed around. It looked like the entire base was abandoned.

That said a lot about the situation of the dragonriders on this base. It didn't seem like they could risk anything. They had launched a full-on assault on the imaginary troll horde. Either Gill had made the situation look extremely dire, or these riders couldn't take any chances.

Alex felt a little bad for having tricked the riders, but it was their own fault. Hopefully, nothing terrible happened while they were out.

The team turned the corner and were greeted by Chine and the rest of the dragons, lazily lounging in the sun. Chine slowly raised his head when he saw Alex, his eyes twinkling in that smile only dragons could do.

The rest of the dragons rose along with Chine. *We were wondering what was taking you so long. Ready to get to work, Dustling?*

CHAPTER THREE

The dragons and the riders split up, each pair making their way toward the stables. The plan was for the dragons to wait outside. It would be easy enough for them to enter once the coast was clear, and Alex wanted to make sure the facility was empty first.

She led the team around the back toward where Gill said the stables were. There was only one entrance from outside, and that was through the specially designed ceiling. The only thing that could get through the ceiling's defense grid was dragons. Anything else would be instantly vaporized.

Instead of going through the ceiling, the team was going to work their way around and sneak in through another section of the facility. They were sending Jollies since she was the smallest, and she was the least likely to get caught after Gill.

Gill would have gone, but he had to keep an eye on the simulation he'd built. The riders of the facility still hadn't come across it and he wasn't sure how long it would hold. The simulation had been enough to get the riders out of the building, but he wasn't sure if it would keep them out there for long enough.

Jollies was making a huge show of getting ready to go into the facility. Her flair for melodrama hadn't lessened, however potentially stressful the situation was. She was demanding that Alex remind her everything was going to be okay.

Alex opened her palm and let Jollies take a seat in it. "Trust me, Jollies, you're the best person for the job," Alex said, wondering how much Jollies needed to hear this.

Jollies sighed, grabbed her hair, and pulled. "But what if I'm not quiet enough? I'm not a sneaky person. Pixies don't sneak. Maybe a fairy would, but not a pixie. What if I get caught? What if I can't find the…what am I looking for again? What if I can't remember what I'm looking for?"

Jollies flashed bright white, then the brightness faded and she looked pale as a sheet of paper. Alex shook her head, smiling. It was evident that the pixie did need the comforting. "Jollies, you'll do okay," Alex whispered. "You're going to head toward HQ and find the mission map."

"How am I going to know what it is?"

That was when Gill spoke up. "The map is going to be in the middle of the HQ war room. It'll be a large, green holographic map. They're usually in the middle of the room. Nearly impossible to miss."

Brath grumbled, "That's if she can remember what she's looking for."

Jollies zipped in front of Brath's face and pulled her dagger. "You bet your ass I'm going to remember!" she growled menacingly.

The rest of the team tried to keep from laughing at how ridiculous Jollies was being.

The pixie flew back to Alex. "All right! I'm ready. Let's do this!"

Jollies slipped under the door leading to the janitor's closet, which opened into the back of the facility to make for simpler waste management. Gill had found it the easiest point in the whole facility to sneak into. The closet was surprisingly large.

Once Jollies was in, she stuck her head under the door that led to the main facility. She was still a long way from the war room, and her best route was going to be through the air ducts. For anyone other than Jollies, it would have been a tight fit. For her, they were downright spacious.

Through the ducts, Jollies made her way toward the war room. The plan was that she would get a copy of the map while the rest of the team tried to find a way to get into the stables.

While Jollies was flying, she was also taking live readings of the areas of the facility she was passing through to make sure there were no other riders. So far, she hadn't come across any.

There was still a good amount of distance between the janitor's closet and the war room, though.

Gill led Team Boundless around the side of the facility, heading for the next section that had a supposed weakness, the gym's bathroom.

Brath was joking about how he hoped that there were enough riders left for them to catch them in the shower. Alex had to cut him off. "Do you know how unbelievably creepy that sounds?" she asked. "Pervy little gnome trying to check out girls in the shower?"

Brath's eyebrows raised with confusion. "Girls?" he asked.

"I'm not trying to see girls in the shower. I wanna see how tough the dudes are. You never get a real fight out of a gnome unless you've burst in on him in the shower. That's the only way you get to see the fire."

Alex turned to Gill and asked, "Is he serious?"

Gill nodded absentmindedly as he checked his HUD visor to make sure they were coming to the right spot. "Oh, yes, quite serious," Gill replied. "It's kind of a game they play, a cultural rite of passage. Of course, these 'fights' are meant to take place under waterfalls, but in the modern setting of Middang3ard, gnomes have expanded this to bathrooms and showers."

Alex was confused. "A cultural thing, huh?" she muttered.

Gill nodded. "All our cultures are strange to others. A drow delicacy is live slugs. And humans love to bleed trees for their desserts."

"Bleed trees?"

"Yes. I believe your kind call it maple syrup."

"But maple syrup is delicious."

Gill gave Alex a blank look. "It's barbaric. The trees have no way to defend themselves."

Alex shrugged as she looked into Gill's eyes. The drow clearly thought the method for making maple syrup was barbaric, and not wanting the conversation to digress into a defense all of humanity for what they slathered on pancakes, she nodded in Brath's direction. "I didn't know that gnomes were so violent. Guess, I always thought that was more of a dwarfish thing."

"Most people think that—until you meet a gnome. Then you realize they're just balls of anger. Makes for interesting friendships, to say the least."

Alex looked at Brath, who was marching along the side of the wall. "Yeah, I imagine it probably does," she mused.

Gill tapped the side of his visor, opening Jollies' channel.

"Hey, how's it coming so far? Are you closing in on the war room?"

Jollies' voice crackled over the headsets of the entire team. "Getting closer. And I haven't come across anyone so far. I think that we might be in the clear. How about you guys?"

"Looks like we're in the clear right now. Nothing—"

Gill stopped talking abruptly. Up ahead, Brath had stopped and was holding up his right hand in a fist, signaling that there was an enemy up ahead. Gill had been right in deciding to take the long route. It would have been foolish to assume the entire facility had been vacated.

Brath joined up with the rest of the team as they moved back. Gill whispered to Jollies, "Be careful, there are definitely people still in the building."

"Got it," Jollies replied. "I'm going dark."

The comm cut out, and the larger portion of Team Boundless moved farther back to plan how they were going to deal with the situation. "We gotta take them out," Brath said. "That's the only way that we're getting past them."

Gill shook his head as he pulled up his visor. "I don't think that is the wisest choice. There could be more than we're expecting. Also, we might face more extreme consequences."

Alex impatiently squirmed. "How much time do we have on that, anyway?" she asked. "That simulation isn't going to last forever."

"You're right. Let me check. Hmm, it looks like we've got a little over half an hour. They still haven't reached the coordinates the simulation is broadcasting."

"What's the best plan of action? We could get in serious trouble for attacking someone, but I don't know how we're going to talk our way into getting in there."

Brath puffed his chest out and slammed his fist to it. "I

got this. You guys don't need to worry about anything. They don't call me Bronze-tongue Brath for nothing."

Alex raised her eyebrow and asked, "Isn't it usually silver or gold tongue?"

"Well, yeah. I'm not the greatest, but I'm a hell of a lot more charismatic than you chumps. Hold on and watch me work my magic."

Before anyone could stop him, Brath walked in the direction of the soldier. Alex hit her face with her palm as she shook her head, and the rest of the team watched. "He really thinks he's the charming one of the group," she muttered.

Brath walked up to the guard and cleared his throat. The guard jumped when the gnome suddenly appeared. "Uh…" the guard said. "Can I help you with something?"

"Yeah, you can," Brath answered. "There's a coolant leak in the basement, and I've been trying to get on the horn with someone. I can't seem to find anybody, but if that leak keeps on going, this whole place is going to lose power."

The guard looked around as if he were going to magically find a senior officer. Brath grunted as the officer tried to figure out what to do. "Yeah, that's what I've been saying," Brath whined. "I can't find anybody. It's like they all went out to lunch or something."

The guard nodded in agreement. "There's an attack, reinforcements for that troll party that got taken care of a little bit back. All hands on deck. There's probably only six or seven of us here right now. Not even a skeleton crew."

"Well, guess that means you six are going to have to take care of that leak. Otherwise, by the time everyone gets back, this place might have already blown sky-high."

"It's that bad?"

"That bad."

Brath pulled up his HUD and scrolled through his inventory until he found a book. He selected it, and the book materialized in his hand. He handed it to the guard. "This here'll show you anything you need to know about coolant leaks. You take care of this, you'll be a hero. Definite promotion."

The guard took the book and looked it over. "Hey, if you know so much about leaks, why don't you take care of it?" he asked.

Brath shook his head as he tapped his noggin. "Would if I could, but this isn't the only leak I've found. I have to keep checking. All I'm saying is I need a hand because I'm not going to be able to patch everything up. I'm just a diagnostics guy."

"All right, all right. Makes sense. I'll get the rest of the guys together and go take care of this. If you run across any other leaks, let us know. Don't want this place falling apart while everyone is out."

The guard walked down the hall as he radioed for the rest of the guards in the facility. Once Brath was certain the guard was out of earshot, he went around the corner and motioned for the rest of the team to come forward.

Alex silently clapped her hands before patting Brath on the back. "I would never have thought you were the one who'd have the gift of gab. I'd upgrade you from bronze to silver."

Brath took a quick bow, his smile a little less smug than usual. The gnome looked like he was genuinely happy with the compliment. "Nice thing about being a gnome is when you start rattling off mechanical jargon, everyone takes your word. Everyone assumes we're always working on their crap."

Gill pointed down the hallway and said, "Come on, this way to the stables."

Brath and the rest of Team Boundless went running down the halls toward the stables, hoping to get there before anyone noticed them, Gill checking his map every couple of seconds just to make sure they didn't run into anyone.

Finally, they arrived at the stables. Alex opened the door, and they stepped through. Her heart sank as she saw the state they were in.

CHAPTER FOUR

The stables were nothing like those in the Wasp's Nest. These seemed to be in complete disrepair. It was hard to tell the last time a dragon had been in the place.

Computer equipment was torn up, and there were cables and internal mechanical pieces all over the floor. It looked like a bomb had gone off inside a massive computer. Alex wasn't certain how she was going to make heads or tails of what to do for Chine.

She had a very limited idea of what changing equipment and maintenance was going to be like. Alex had only seen the equipment attached before. She hadn't gotten to the part of training where she was taught how to detach anything.

Boundless wandered around the stables. All the other members looked confused by the state of the stables as well. "Isn't this a dragonriders' facility?" Jim wondered out loud. "How the hell do they take care of their dragons with every-thing so…busted up?"

Brath leaned over the side of the area that the dragons were usually kept. It didn't look like anything had been there for some time. "Maybe they don't have any dragons," Brath suggested. "This place looks like it hasn't been used for years."

Alex tapped one of the computers and then hit its power button. The machine remained off. "That's probably why they aren't mounting a rescue party for Roy and Toppinir—they don't have the resources. I thought they were just being jerks. How did this happen?"

Gill sat down in the control center of the stables. "No idea, but it isn't good. It couldn't have been funding. Myrddin has a nearly infinite budget. Perks of being an alchemist. Whatever happened here must have been something else. Who knows? We should focus on our situation."

"You're right. Let's get this sorted out."

Alex reached out telepathically to Chine. *Where are you guys?*

A mighty roar ripped through the air. Alex looked up at the opening in the ceiling. The dragons were flying overhead. They zoomed down into the stables, gracefully separating and taking up residence in the augment section of the stables. "Gill, can you get this stuff back online?" Alex asked.

Gill took a look at the main computer of the control center and sighed. "Yeah, I probably can. Might take a bit of time, but I'll get it running."

Alex hit her comm and patched to Jollies. "Hey, girl, how's the search going?" she asked.

Jollies' voice came through the comm, frantic and panicked. "I'm in the war room, but there isn't a holograph. I can't find it. I'm going to fail the only mission I have!"

"Hey, hey, calm down. Hold on; we'll figure this out."

Alex ran over to Chine and jumped down into his resting spot. The dragon rose when he saw her. *Hey, Chine, can you do me a favor?*

Chine stretched out his wings slowly as he nodded. *What do you need?*

Jollies' eyes. She's having a hard time finding what she's looking for. Maybe if she had an extra set of eyes, it could help her out.

Chine closed his eyes, and Alex took that as a yes. She came over to the dragon, sat down beneath his wings, and closed her eyes.

Alex felt a tickling behind her eyeballs, a soft scratching like something was moving around in the back of her skull. When she opened her eyes, she was no longer in the stables. Everything around her was moving very fast—far too fast to make any sense of it. "Hey, Jollies, slow down," Alex shouted.

Jollies froze, or at least, Alex thought that she had stopped moving. Alex's viewpoint had at least stopped moving. "Uh, Alex?" Jollies asked.

"Don't worry about anything. I'm just looking through your eyes so I can give you a hand finding the holograph map. That's all."

"Wait, you're looking through my eyes? How many fingers am I holding up?"

Alex couldn't see Jollies' fingers and chuckled. "Jollies, you have to look at your fingers for me to see them."

Jollies laughed nervously and said, "Oh, okay." She raised her hand in front of her eyes, holding up three fingers.

"Three fingers. Now can we get started? And fly slow. I'm not used to looking through your eyes."

Jollies started to fly around the room, moving slower. "This is so weird," Jollies admitted. "Are you in my head or something? Can you read my mind?"

"No, I'm just seeing through your eyes. It's a psychic link, but I don't think I can read your mind or anything like that."

Chine's thoughts broke through Alex's. *Not yet, but with practice, your psychic powers might be as strong as mine one day.*

Alex did a double-take, switching back to her own eyes for a moment so she could see Chine. *Wait, what? Are you saying I have psychic powers?*

Didn't Myrddin tell you? That's why our connection is so strong. The spell Myrddin crafted for you was not merely new eyes. It's a psychic link, which means you have psychic powers. The beginnings, at least. They need to be worked, like a muscle.

Alex was giddy about the idea, but she figured she'd come back to that later. The mission needed to be their priority. "All right, Jollies, we're looking for a giant holomap. Can you take a look around so I can get a better view?"

Jollies and Alex slowly scanned the war room. Like the stables, the war room looked like it hadn't been used much in ages. What had happened to this facility?

It was obvious where the holographic map was supposed to be. There was a large platform in the middle of the room where it would have been projected. It would have been easy for everyone in the room to see it from that vantage point.

"That's where it should be," Alex said. "That spot right there."

Jollies flew to the platform and looked around, taking her time when Alex reminded the pixie that she needed to concentrate on not moving too fast. Alex could see the spot had been outfitted for a projection. "Hey, Jollies, can you test the lights in the room?"

Jollies replied, "Sure," as she zoomed over to the light switch on the wall. She flipped the switch. The lights remained off.

Alex switched back to her own eyes, jumped up, and leaped back into the main section of the stables. "Hey! Gill! Is the electricity running to this room?"

Gill whirled around from the computer he was tinkering with. "Let me check," he replied as he pulled up his HUD visor. After a couple of seconds, he pushed his visor back down and said, "Nope! It looks like most of the power's being routed to other parts of the facility."

"Route the power back to this room and to the war room.

That should fix Jollies' problem, at least."

Gill flashed Alex a thumbs-up and started messing around on his dragon anchor. After a couple of seconds, the power cut back on, and the lights turned on in the stables.

Alex closed her eyes and concentrated until she felt the tickle in the back of her head. When she opened her eyes, she was seeing through Jollies' eyes, and she was looking at a bright green holographic map. "Perfect," Alex said. "Jollies, can you upload the map to your dragon anchor? Along with any important information?"

Jollies nodded, disorienting Alex. "Yeah, I can manage that."

"Let me know if you have any more problems. Head back to the stables after you get it."

Alex returned to her own vision. "All right, Jollies has the map," Alex told everyone. "Now all we have to do is get these dragons taken care of. How are things going, Gill?"

Gill stood up from the computer system, sighing and shaking his head. His face looked grim. "Not good. Even with power routed to the stables, we aren't going to have enough to get any of the augment stations working."

"Can you explain what that means in English?"

Gill jumped down onto the main platform of the stables. "It means we can remove what we've put on our dragons, but we aren't going to be able to replace the weapons—and that creates a problem. The longer those augments are on our dragons, the more damage there's going to be."

"Wait, what? I thought if we did the maintenance, it wasn't going—"

"That's not how it works. The augments aren't meant to stay on for extended periods of time. That's why you have to do maintenance."

Alex threw her hands up in frustration as she paced. "Okay, Gill, I'm hearing a lot of problems, but I'm not hearing any solutions," she moaned. "I just don't know enough about this stuff."

Gill placed his hand on Alex's shoulder and smiled at her reassuringly. "We aren't screwed," he said. "The power's back on. We can still take care of the dragons, and I'll work at seeing if I can get any more systems back online. Until then, though, you're going to have to get your hands dirty."

The rest of the dragonriders had come over to Alex and Gill. As Gill was preparing to speak, Jollies rushed through the door, almost flying into Alex's face. "I got the map!" she squeaked.

Alex gave Jollies a high five and said, "That's great," as Gill cleared his throat to speak. "Oh, sorry, didn't mean to steal your thunder," Alex apologized.

Gill replied, "You didn't. And it wasn't going to be an exciting statement. Have any of you performed maintenance on your dragons before?"

None of the team said anything. Gill sighed. "Have any of you read through the manual on performing maintenance? Did any of you do any research after our initial lessons?"

More silence. Brath awkwardly coughed, which only made the silence more uncomfortable. "All right," Gill went on. "It's going to be pretty simple. You're going to use your dragon anchors to drain the draconian fluid from where the augments rest on your dragon's skin. The fluid will be stored in your anchor. The fluid has a myriad of different—"

Alex interrupted Gill, saying, "Uh, do we really need the science lesson right now? How about you give us the Cliffs-Notes so we can get up and running."

Gill nodded and continued, "All right, you're going to drain the fluid, store it in your anchor, and reattach the augments. If I can get the system going, we'll put some new ones on, but it's unnecessary. They'll be good after being drained. We should get to it."

The riders split up, looking for their dragons in the stables, which didn't take long. Alex jumped down into Chine's holding area and reached out to his mind. *So, you know the drill, right?* she asked.

Chine raised his wings as he stood, allowing Alex easier access to his chest and claw augments. *Ah, yes, my favorite part of my service to the realms—being taken care of and groomed like common livestock.*

Alex approached Chine and stood in front of his chest. She looked down at her dragon anchor, uncertain of how she was going to detach Chine's armor and how she was going to scoop out the draconian fluid.

Waiting was unnecessary, though, because Alex's dragon anchor began to glow the same color as the flashing green light on Chine's chest piece. Alex reached out to the blinking light.

The chest piece contorted, plates of steel rolling back. It was the same kind of nano-tech Alex's armor was made from. The chest piece created a hole the size of Alex's wrist. "I put my hand in there?" Alex asked.

Chine nodded as Alex curled her bottom lip. "Am I putting my hand...in *you?*" Alex asked.

"Yes, into my chest. It's the easiest way to drain my fluids. It'll allow the augment to continue sitting there without my blood burning and searing the piece to my flesh."

"Jeez, sounds terrible."

"The first generation of dragons sacrificed a lot so we'd have the technology we do today. Their sacrifices should never be forgotten."

Alex took a deep breath and plunged her hand into Chine's chest. The dragon winced as Alex felt her dragon anchor start to warm up. It went quickly from warm to searing. Alex almost screamed in pain, and the dragon growled under his breath.

If she hadn't been so concerned with Chine's well-being, she would have pulled her arm out as soon as it had started to get uncomfortable. But this was necessary to keep Chine's blood from melting the armor into his skin. This was her part.

Alex could feel the heat traveling from her skin to her bone. It felt like her entire skeleton was catching on fire. And then it was suddenly gone. She pulled her anchor out, and the chest augment settled back into place.

Chine shook his wings and huffed out a cloud of black smoke. "Just five more times," he grumbled. "Save the neck anchor for last. It's the most painful."

Alex nodded as she got started, working her way through each anchor, draining the draconian fluid. Her skin took fire, then her bones, the heat boiling up in her body to such a degree she felt like she was aflame on the inside. Then, just as quickly as it started, nothing.

After she had drained all of the lower augments, she climbed up on top of Chine and raised her hand above his anchor. Her anchor and the dragon's started to blink in rhythm, then a hole opened up on his back. Alex knelt and plunged her arm into it.

Chine let out a roar of pain as he flinched. Alex felt the fire shoot up her arm, faster than it had before. Flames were burning behind her eyes. There was no feeling in her arm. It was as if it had been dissolved. Then Alex felt her arm being forced out of the hole.

Skin and scales grew over the wound until the nanotech covered everything. Alex leaped off Chine's back as the dragon reached up and stretched. "Glad that's finally over," he said. "Now we just need to wait for the rest of them.

Alex took a seat next to him. She felt sick to her stomach, and the world went black at the edge of her vision. Even though she fought it, she slipped into a deep sleep.

CHAPTER FIVE

Alex felt like she'd been sleeping for a lifetime, but when she woke up, hardly any time had passed. Chine had nudged her awake, and now she lay staring at the sky through the open ceiling of the stables. *What happened?* Alex asked.

The dragon curled his tail around Alex to prop her up. *A side effect of our mental link, your latent psychic abilities, and the draconian fluid.*

You know, just because you're using words, it doesn't mean you're making sense. How about we try again, but you assume I don't know how any of that works?

Chine chuckled before he started speaking again. *The anchor has to do something with the fluid. It recirculates through your body and processes it as waste. But there are some riders who have different effects. You seem to be one of them. And that means the draconian fluid, or dragon's blood, as it should properly be called, makes you stronger, akin to the dragon-blooded of old. You might be the closest we've had to one in a long while, but don't let it go to your head. It just means our bond will be stronger."*

Alex yawned as she stretched, still trying to shake off her

sudden sleep. *Well, that's good to know, I guess. How's everyone else finishing up?*

Chine reached out telepathically to the rest of the dragons, and after a few moments, told Alex all the dragonriders had finished their maintenance. Jim had finished working on his mech a while ago. "Okay," Alex said. "Guess it's time to get moving."

Alex walked out of Chine's area and approached Gill, who was still tinkering with the central computer system. "No luck getting it online?" Alex asked.

Gill turned to face Alex. He looked exhausted. Apparently, the maintenance process had been hard on him, too. For all his book knowledge, the drow had been unprepared for the reality of taking care of their dragons. "No, not the entire system, but I was able to glean more information from the system using the map Jollies brought. Our coordinates are all entered and updated to our links."

Jim, Brath, and Jollies walked up to Alex and Gill, looking pretty beat. It would have been nice to have a moment for everyone to catch their breath. Jim was the only one who looked ready to go, but he was the only one who didn't have to process the dragons' blood.

Alex sat down next to Gill. "Maybe we should all just chill for a little—"

An alarm blared through the stables as the power came back on. Bright red lights flashed as a voice shouted over the intercom, "Intruders! Intruders! The stables are compromised. Security on the way."

Gill leaned over the computer, trying to see what could have tripped the alarm. "Damn it," he muttered. "I must have brought the security system back on when I was going through the map."

"Well, forget chilling, then! We need to ride!"

Team Boundless each went to their own dragon. Alex

leaped down into Chine's stables, landed on his back, raised her anchor, and then they were off, soaring into the sky as the alarms blared behind them.

Alex looked over her shoulder, giddy with the fright of having almost been caught. "Hell, yeah!" she exclaimed. "Guess your plan went off without a hitch, Gill! Dude, you are a freakin' miracle."

Gill, who was flying beside Alex, smiled softly as he nodded. "Thank you. It is appreciated."

Brath groaned loudly enough to be heard over the wind and without the comm. "You two could use a private channel, you know," Brath suggested.

A laser beam shot past Alex, burning a little bit of her hair. "Holy crap!" she shouted as she turned.

A horde of drones was pouring out of the stables, heading for the riders. The drones were nearly the size of a gnome, but it wasn't their size that worried her. It was the sheer number of them. There seemed to be dozens.

Jim's voice crackled over his older comm system. He was laughing as he spoke. "Looks like Gill the Nerd brought a hell storm on us," he chided.

Gill laughed too. "If you can't deal with a couple of drones, maybe you shouldn't be riding with Boundless."

Over the comm, Brath muttered, "Gods, you two should just get a room already. Alex, what's the plan?"

Alex pointed to a nearby mountain range. "We can lose them in the mountains. Maybe not Jim, though. Jim, can you keep up with us if we hit top speed?"

He answered, "There's no way I'm going to be able to match your speed. The mech is too slow."

"Jollies, you and I are going to run a distraction. The rest of you, cover Jim and head to the mountains."

Jollies flashed Alex a smile as the two of them peeled off from the rest of the riders, who sped toward the mountain range, making sure to slow down for Jim's hulking dragon mech.

Alex and Jollies went straight for the drones, using their superior speed to weave out of the way of the lasers. The drones seemed to take a long time to lock onto a target, especially if the target was moving. Alex didn't need to say anything to Jollies. The pixie zipped and zoomed as fast as she could.

They were still a good distance from the drones, and the air was already beginning to thicken with heat from the lasers. "Do you think we're going to get busted for this?" Jollies shouted.

Alex swerved to the left, barely avoiding a missile that had flown at her. "If we survive this, we might be in a little bit of trouble," She laughed.

"You have a really bad habit of getting involved in suicide missions."

Chine pulled up, absorbing one of the lasers with his chest piece before launching an ether fire ball at the drone that had made the mistake of hitting him. "You know, I'm pretty sure we've been on a suicide mission since we first got here," Alex said. "At least we chose this one."

Alex and Jollies dived farther into the exploding field of lasers and drones. They were close enough now so the drones were having an even harder time aiming. The drones had been built for long-range combat, and the closer the riders got, the less effective the devices became.

Heading toward the mountain range might not have been the best idea, in hindsight. It would give the drones the advantage. Further, it would funnel the drones into a tight space with the riders, making the range a shooting gallery for whoever got lucky.

Alex determined that it was going to be the riders. She just had to figure out how to ensure they had the advantage.

A drone larger than the rest broke away from the swarm. It was covered in multiple sensors and eyes. The drone did not attack, just popped out of the swarm and watched. "I don't like the look of that thing," Alex shouted. "Jollies, can you handle it?"

Jollies didn't answer but surged forward, working her way around the other drones with a skill far beyond her years and stopping abruptly in front of the drone. She aimed her dragon anchor, and Timber let loose a crack of lightning that split the drone in half.

Alex was flying through the swarm now, the drones trying to figure out the best way to attack. There didn't seem to be one. Chine was tearing through the drones, and Alex had pulled out her scythe to help cut them down. However, the drones kept coming.

Jollies and Alex pulled up out of the swarm, flying backward so they could keep an eye on the drones. The devices seemed to have lost interest in the other riders. That was good news.

Then the drones did something that alarmed Alex greatly. The drones all stopped together. It was as if they had all received the same order and responded to it at precisely the same time. The drones stayed perfectly still, their red eyes blinking like a stalling computer.

Alex leaned over Chine's neck to get a better look. "This isn't good. I've seen this happen before; I just don't know where. But I've seen this. I know I have."

Then it clicked. It was the same uniform movement Alex had seen with her dragon armor. The drones were starting to move like nanotech. That was a *very* bad thing.

As if the drones were reading Alex's mind, they melded together, pressing against each other so tightly you couldn't see where one drone ended and the next began. They formed a complex chain of robot bodies, taking the shape of a cobra.

The drone snake was easily twice the size of Chine. The only dragon on Team Boundless large enough to deal with the drone cobra was Furi, but he was too far ahead with Jim and the rest.

Alex didn't need to tell Chine what to do. The dragon had already picked it up. He fired another fireball as he retreated, heading toward the mountain range, Jollies racing at his side. *Can't say I've seen that before,* Chine murmured.

Alex chuckled. *Really? Aren't you dragons supposed to have seen it all by now?*

I am still young and new to battle. This is a first.

Alex always forgot Chine was still considered to be a young dragon and didn't have much combat experience. Sometimes he said things that made Alex think he was as green as she was, but his combat skills suggested otherwise. Maybe dragons were born with an innate understanding of fighting.

Jollies and Alex raced toward the mountain range. Alex tried to reach the other riders by comm, but there must have been too much distance between them, or the drones were blocking the transmission. At this point, it didn't matter.

The pressing issue was the giant nanotech cobra hissing and shooting lasers at Jollies and Alex.

Going into the mountain range was an almost guaranteed death trap now. When the drones were just a horde, they would have been easy enough to scatter. Now that they had formed a whole creature, they seemed to have grown bolder and more aggressive.

On top of that issue, if there were any cracks in the mountain range Team Boundless could have exploited, they would be useless now. The drone cobra was too large. It would dominate the space.

Alex couldn't think of a reasonable course of action, other than linking back up with the rest of the team. So far, Alex's usual plan was to attack and hope things worked themselves out. This time, it was obvious attacking the techno-cobra was not going to work out.

Alex's comm started to buzz and she flipped up her HUD to see who it was. Manny's unhappy eyes met hers. "I do not have time for this right now," she muttered as she hung up on Manny.

He's probably just going to tell me in a thousand different ways how I should have stayed at the facility. And I do not have time for that.

The techno-cobra let out a roar that reminded Alex she did *not* have time to talk to Manny. As she looked over her shoulder, she could see it opening its mouth, a bright red light glowing in the back of its throat. "It's charging for a blast!" Alex shouted.

Jollies and Alex broke away from each other as a laser blast seared past them, carving a gash into the side of the mountains ahead. "That thing is no joke!" Jollies shouted.

Alex pointed up and started to ascend, heading straight into the clouds. Jollies followed her as she patched into Gill. "Hey! Hypothetically speaking, if there were a giant nanotech snake following us, would you have any idea how to disable it?" she asked.

Gill's voice crackled over the comm. "Hypothetically speaking, Jim should have an EMP device in his dragon mech that would disable any electronics that aren't dragon-forged," he answered.

"Is that true, Jim?"

Jim replied confidently, "Yeah, I have a couple of EMP devices. A bomb, even. The mechs come outfitted with a dozen different EMP weapons."

"Are you ready to play the hero today?"

"I was born ready."

CHAPTER SIX

Alex and Jollies rose higher as the cobra followed on their tails. They were biding their time, trying to put some space between themselves and the cobra while Jim told them his coordinates.

Surprisingly, the rest of the team had found an almost invisible cavern in one of the mountains. Brath had had the great idea of hiding there for an ambush.

The only problem was, Jollies and Alex needed enough space between them and the nanotech cobra so they could surprise the machine creature.

A laser blast tore past Alex, who pulled hard to the left on Chine, swinging up higher to avoid the blast. "Are we getting any farther ahead of them?" Alex shouted.

Jollies checked over her shoulder and shook her head. "It looks like it's gaining on us," Jollies replied. "Oh, wait! I have an idea. Gill said an EMP would disable them, right? Amber can create her own electromagnetism. Hold on!"

Jollies started to weave back and forth in front of Alex. Every couple of seconds, Amber would drop what looked like a small glowing ball. Every so often, a crack of lightning would snap around the ball—tiny EMP grenades.

As the techno-cobra sped after the dragonriders, it bumped into the first mini-EMP grenade. The grenade went off, sending a chain reaction of exploding EMPs through the sky.

The techno-cobra shrieked in what sounded like pain as its body started to come apart. Drones flew in different directions, confused by the energy coming off the grenades. Their communication was severed. It would take some time to re-establish a link.

Jollies and Alex flew down under the clouds as fast as they could toward the coordinates of the rest of the team. They sped through the mountains until they found the cavern where the team was huddled.

The cave was a huge gash in a slope, with enough space to fit at least two more full-sized dragons. Chine and Amber were easily able to fit into the remaining space. There was even enough room for the riders to walk around beneath their dragons.

As Alex leaped off Chine, Jim's mechanical mech moved toward the lip of the gash and plopped down. The back opened up, and Jim pulled himself out of the mech. Gill came up and gave Jim a hand climbing down from the mech. "And now for the final touch," Gill said.

Timber turned around so his tail was facing out toward the other mountains. He spread his wings over the gap, blocking out the light, so only a little bit got through. Then his scales shimmered and changed color and texture to that of the mountain.

Team Boundless was completely camouflaged from the outside. Even to a drone, they would look the same as the mountain's slopes. Now all they had to do was wait for the drones to come through. "Wait, Jollies and I lost them. How do we know they're coming?" Alex asked.

Jim jerked his thumb at his mech. "We figured out how they were tracking us," Jim said. "All mech riders have a transponder on their rig. Mine's no different. Unfortunately, it isn't something we're told. Guess they think we might run off on some stupid mission with them."

"And they send drones after you to kill you?"

"Probably not. We all saw that facility wasn't up to snuff. It's probably a malfunction. Murder seems a little extreme for a joyride. Either way, Gill and Brath helped me cut out the transponder. We're still leaving it running for a little bit to draw the drones in, then Gill's got something planned for it."

Gill had gone to sit down on a rock, folding one leg over the other. He closed his eyes as he meditated. Alex wanted to ask him what he was planning, but once Gill closed his eyes, he was dead to the world until he opened them.

Jollies landed on Alex's shoulder as she walked over to Brath and took a seat beside him. "How are you holding up?" she asked.

Brath forced a smile from beneath his beard. "It feels weird to be disobeying orders like this," Brath admitted. "I mean, you'd think they would want us to help them instead of trying to shove us in the barracks."

Alex shrugged. "They just don't know what we're capable of," she said. "People tend to underestimate me, don't you think?"

Brath nodded as Alex winked at him and laughed. "Yeah," the gnome said. "I have firsthand experience of that. So, what, we just wait here forever?"

"Better than being out there, hunted by that freaky cobra thing. Trust me, you'd rather be bored for a little bit than have to deal with that."

Team Boundless waited, occasionally standing and stretching, walking back and forth to kill time. Gill was the only one who didn't seem bothered. Everyone else, especially Alex, looked ready to come out of their skin.

Because of Timber's cloaking, the team wasn't able to check if the drones were coming. All they could do was look at Jim's computer system, the blinking green lights in a green graph. Something was coming, at least, but only Jim really knew how far away it was at the moment.

Alex wandered over to where Chine was relaxing, plopped down next to him, and curled up under his wing. *I haven't heard you complain about how bored you are in a whole day,* the dragon joked.

Chine's scales rose and settled back down as Alex nuzzled up closer. *I'm trying to get better about that. It makes it harder for everyone else if I'm complaining all the time too. Waiting shouldn't be torture. I mean, look at Gill."*

The dragon raised his head and looked across the snug hiding spot at Gill, who was now meditating on top of Timber's head. He chuckled. *Patient dragon. That would drive me crazy.*

So, does everyone talk to their dragon as much as I talk to you? It's kinda weird—you know, everyone sitting in a room quietly, having conversations no one can hear.

Chine absentmindedly clawed at the ground underneath him. *The older dragons used to speak aloud. Their language was of the elements. That's all breathing fire is—speaking the old tongue. We young ones, though, haven't mastered the art. For us, speaking could accidentally kill you. Best to err on the side of caution.*

Damn, you guys really are that powerful? Gets me thinking again. What the hell could the Dark One have that's bigger and tougher than you dragons?

I do not know. No doubt, we will find out soon enough.

Alex's comm went off, beeping loudly, potentially giving

away their position. She covered it quickly and answered the call. It was Manny. "What do you want, Manny?" she hissed. "This isn't the best time for me to talk."

Before Manny spoke, Alex patched their conversation into the team channel. Gill opened his eyes as Jim, Brath, and Jollies walked over to Alex.

Manny was practically shouting at the top of his lungs. "I know it's not a good time for you to be talking since I know you have a horde of drones after you! What were you thinking? Do you know how much trouble you're going—"

"I don't care how much trouble I'm getting into. Did you hear about Roy and Toppinir? Absolutely no backup, and they aren't getting any unless we bring it to them."

Manny sighed loudly, and Alex could imagine the look on his face. She'd seen it enough through Manny's eyes. "Okay, I know it sounds bad, but they're figuring something out. I still don't know what it is, but they're working on… Oh, I don't know, Alex," he admitted.

"I knew it!" Alex exclaimed. "You guys have no idea how to help them."

"Wait, wait. I'm not the one in charge of planning anything. All I get is the information that's passed to me. They may have—"

"Manny, tell me the truth. Are they planning on saving Roy and Toppinir?"

Manny was silent for a long time, much longer than needed. Alex already knew the answer. She just wanted to hear Manny say it. "They aren't planning on sending any backup," Manny finally said. "Roy and Toppinir are too far into enemy territory. We'd lose tons of riders getting there."

Alex crossed her arms, trying to remember she wasn't angry with Manny. None of this was his fault. He was trying to look out for her and the whole team. His only mistake was caring about Alex. "That's why we have to do this," she explained, "I know we can get him out. I recognized where they are. From VR."

"You have to be kidding me. You think you can save him because you remember an area from VR? Do you know how insane that sounds?"

"Not as insane as letting your two best dragonriders get killed by the Dark One."

Manny laughed, which surprised Alex. "It's almost as insane as letting our most promising new recruits throw their lives away on a suicide mission," he countered.

"Good point. We're still going. So, either help keep us alive or stop wasting our time."

Manny sighed again, and Alex could have sworn he was going to hang up on her. "I wish your personality profile had mentioned how stubborn you are. I'll call you if I find anything out that'll help you. Be careful, Alex."

"Thanks, Manny. You too."

Gill leaped off Timber and joined the rest of the team around Alex. "Sounds straightforward enough." The drow glowered. "They're just planning on abandoning them."

Jollies zipped around, shaking her head. "It's not that simple. It's a death mission. Oh, sorry, a *suicide* mission. You heard what Manny said. They'd lose too many people."

Brath didn't seem to care how many people would be lost. He was brooding underneath his beard. "It's cowardly," he finally spat. "Those two are practically heroes, and they're just going to leave them."

Jim rested his hand on Brath's shoulder. "Roy's my captain. Since I became a mech rider, all I've heard is how he and Toppinir are unstoppable. Myrddin probably thinks they're going to pull their asses out of this like they always do."

Brath pushed off Jim's hand. "Have they come out of anything this bad before?"

Alex had to interject here. "Honestly, we don't even know how bad it is," she admitted. "I mean, we know that they say it's a suicide mission, but we're kinda scant on the details. Maybe Manny's right. We're flying in the dark here."

There was a loud beep, and Alex checked her HUD—a message from Manny. It read, "Big briefing in a few minutes about Roy and Toppinir. Find out if you can *see* anything. Be safe."

Alex could read between the lines. More importantly, Manny thought this was worth supporting. She knew that if Manny didn't think it was possible, he wouldn't have bothered sending her this. It was a sign of faith—a pallid sign, but a sign nonetheless.

"Scratch that," Alex said. "Manny's with us. What else do you need?"

Jim's mech started shrieking a beep three times louder than the one that had gone off on Alex's HUD. "Obviously to pay attention to the swarm of drones heading toward us," Jim shouted as he ran to his mech.

Jim jumped in and closed the cockpit behind him. The mech rose to its feet and lumbered over to the mouth of the cave. "Gill, I'm going to need a visual from you for when to fire," he shouted.

Gill climbed onto Timber's wing and poked his head out of the cave.

The swarm of drones had recombined into the nanotech cobra and it was heading right toward the cave. "Oh, I can see why you said this was a problem," he murmured before returning to the cave and shouting, "Fire in five!"

Jim flipped through a couple of holographic menus in his mech before finding the manual switch for the EMP bomb. He flipped the switch and positioned his mech so its mouth was facing out of the cave.

As the swarm of drones flew past, Jim pulled the EMP

lever and a glowing ball of electromagnetic energy flew out of the mech's mouth into the middle of the swarm of drones. The bomb detonated instantly, and a pulse of energy rocked the drones.

There was no physical damage, but the drones shook for a second before shutting off and falling out of the sky.

Jim pulled his mech back into the cave. "I'll now respond to either 'hero' or 'savior of the day,'" he said, smiling as Gill gave him a high five and Brath scowled approvingly. "Whatever makes you feel more comfortable. I prefer 'savior.'"

Alex punched Jim on the shoulder on her way to Chine. She didn't want to make his head any bigger, though it was good to see him finally start acting like himself in front of the other riders. He was almost like the Jim she had played with in VR, if a little more serious.

Alex reached out telepathically to Chine. *Hey, how strong can you boost my ability to see through someone else's eyes?*

Chine answered, *Substantially. But you may not need my help. If you're trying to reach Manny, you may be able to do it on your own.*

How?

As I said, your psychic powers show potential. We should work on honing them. For now, concentrate on Manny. Try to imagine him in your mind's eye. Once you can see him, focus on seeing through him, then open your eyes. But you must concentrate. Push everything else from your mind.

Alex closed her eyes. She pushed every thought in her head away. Ignored Gill's cute butt. Tried not to think of Brath's endless pacing, or whether or if Jollies felt comfortable around her. Forgot about her parents. Myrddin ceased to exist. The only thing in the universe was Manny's eyes.

When Alex reopened her eyes, they were the foggy green of Manny's. She watched what Manny watched, trying to memorize everything she saw. She let Manny's many eyes flood her with information and concentrated on every moving thing. When Manny left the room, Alex closed her eyes and returned to her own sight.

Above, Brath had finally gotten tired of waiting. "All right, we should just go! We have the coordinates," he complained.

Alex whistled for the attention of the other riders. "Oh, trust me, we're going. But now I have a plan."

CHAPTER SEVEN

Gill uploaded the coordinates Jollies had stolen from the facilities war room, and Team Boundless was off. Alex still hadn't explained the plan to the rest of the team, but she knew what had to be done. She had seen what kind of fight they were headed toward through Manny's eyes.

Every second spent talking and explaining was wasting time they needed. Alex just hoped she had the trust of her team. That was the most important thing at the moment. She hadn't had much time to prove herself to them, but she didn't think she'd disappointed them so far. Today wasn't going to be any different.

Alex kept Team Boundless close to the ground as they flew away from the mountains, heading toward a green valley. Beyond the valley was a dying forest, trees gnarled and breaking apart, roots lifted from the ground, fighting for life.

Gill and Brath were having a hard time flying that close to the ground. Their dragon's claws kept scraping it, slowing them down. Brath was getting audibly more annoyed, grumbling loudly and not bothering to turn his comm down.

Jollies and Jim, on the other hand, weren't having a problem. Amber was small enough that it didn't matter what height she was flying at; her speed was not affected. And Jim's mech seemed to be able to take whatever you threw at it. The thing wasn't fast, but it was stout.

Alex didn't mind the closeness to the ground. She hadn't noticed it, but she often took her flying skills for granted. It hadn't crossed her mind that the other riders might have trouble staying so low without losing speed. That was something she'd have to keep in mind for the future. What good was trying to lead if you forgot about what everyone needed?

Brath's voice broke through Alex's musings. "Okay, I'm just going to say, this is idiotic," he grumbled. "Why the hell are we staying so low? There's a whole sky above us. And last time I checked, we were riding dragons, not horses."

Gill sighed over the intercom. "For once, I am going to have to agree with Brath," he joined in. "It makes no sense to be this low to the ground. We are moving slower and less efficiently."

Alex countered, "Not everyone is moving slower. You two just need to concentrate and keep up."

When Brath spoke, you could hear the sting in his voice. "'Just concentrate and keep up?'" he repeated. "Not all of us are riding micro-dragons. Furi is huge! Do you know how much it takes just to keep him from nosediving into the ground right now?"

"That's not what, I mean, Brath. Sorry. I just meant, if you pay attention to—"

"Trust me, I'm friggin' paying attention."

Alex took a deep breath as she tried to find the right words. She was doing that thing where she got flustered and tried to explain herself. The right words just didn't come.

In fact, they were the exact opposite; they were the wrong words. Most of the time, Alex felt like she could convey her thoughts and ideas to other people, but every so often, she started to stick her foot in her mouth and forgot how to pull it out.

"Just because you have some freakish gift and are an amazing rider who doesn't have any problem doing anything other than impressing everyone around you—"

Brath had gone off the deep end. He was ranting faster than Alex could listen. Luckily, the rest of Boundless wasn't patched into the channel because it would have been embarrassing for everyone. Brath was really letting her have it.

Part of Alex wanted to say that this tirade was just him being insecure—projecting his worries and fears onto her—but she knew that wasn't true. This plan hadn't considered anyone's comfort or skill level other than her own. Brath had every right to be upset.

The best thing to do was listen—to hear him out and let the gnome get everything off of his chest. Hopefully, that wouldn't take too long. Besides, they still had a ways to go.

Before they had left, Alex had gone over the map and its coordinates with the whole team. The initial route they had planned would have brought Boundless to Toppinir's and Roy's location within thirty minutes. It would have been a straight shot.

After seeing through Manny's eyes, Alex thought it was a bad idea to take the direct route. She wanted to go a more roundabout way, maintaining that staying low was the most important thing, regardless of how long it was going to take.

Initially, everyone had thought it was a bad idea. After a few minutes of arguing, they still thought it was a bad idea, but it was Alex's idea. They had decided to trust her.

Now Gill was pinging Alex on top of Brath. Alex told Brath to hold on and answered Gill. "Yeah, what's up?"

"Why are you having us stay so low?" Gill asked. "It doesn't make any sense."

"Oh, my God, you too?"

"Would you prefer we follow you blindly? We're a team, and I am not going to follow without being given a good reason."

Gill had a point. Expecting everyone to listen to her without giving them a reason wasn't the best idea. Alex had figured it would be a waste of time to go over every detail of her plan, but now, it seemed like at least two of her riders were doubting her judgment. "Okay, hold on, Gill," Alex said before switching back to Brath, who was still ranting.

Alex combined Gill's and Brath's comms and then patched the rest of the team into the conversation. Brath continued ranting until he was breathless and panting. "Okay, Brath," Alex said. "I'd prefer you didn't use that language about me, but I can see you're mad."

Brath let out an exasperated shout. "You're damn right, I'm mad. What the hell are we even doing?" he shouted.

Jim stepped in. "Just hold on, Brath. Alex is one of the best strategists I've ever played with. We can trust her."

"That you've *played* with? Excuse me for remembering this is not a human VR game, and so far, all of Alex's *strategies*, if you want to call them that have been, have been to rush in and try not to die."

Alex was stung by Brath's words. What came next hurt even more. "Brath has a point," Gill seconded. "Many of Alex's plans have relied on her extreme skill, placing the rest of us at risk if we couldn't keep up. I'd like to know this isn't another one of those."

Jim chuckled as he shook his head. "Okay, guys, are you listening to yourselves? Alex has been doing great so far. That's why we're here right now."

"Exactly. That is why we are riding into what could be a death trap with little or no understanding of our odds or why we are taking such an impractical route."

The comm went silent. Gill's cold logic was much more painful than Brath's boisterous complaining. Gill had hit the nail dead on the head. Then a voice cut through the comm. It was Jollies. "That's not true," she squeaked.

Gill took a deep breath and said, "Please explain to me where my argument is faulty."

"Alex has been making tough calls. She got us out of the Nest because she was willing to take risks. It has nothing to do with ignoring what we're capable of. She's willing to risk it all, and that's what's gotten us this far. And that's what's going to save Roy and Toppinir."

No one replied. Alex was surprised and glad Jollies had spoken up. It was all Alex needed to be reminded of what she was doing. She was making a call, and it was the right one. "Trust me, guys," Alex said. "I'm not going to ask you to do anything crazy."

Brath scoffed and countered, "Anything crazier than what you're already asking, right?"

"Right. Nothing crazier. Now come on. We're getting closer. We need to focus."

Alex took the lead, pushing Chine ahead of the others. The dragonriders followed, Jollies moving up toward the front with Alex. They looked at each other briefly, and Jollies smiled brightly. "Thanks, Jollies," Alex said gratefully.

Jollies' smile brightened as her body shimmered yellow. "No problem," she said. "You see things we don't. I get it."

That was when Alex remembered Manny. He was close to where the action was happening. She mentally told Chine to keep going in the same direction as she closed her eyes and focused on seeing through Manny.

Alex slid into darkness for a second, but when she opened her eyes, she was seeing through Manny's many eyes. She took the situation in. It was worse than she'd expected from her first viewing, but it wasn't anything Boundless couldn't handle.

Slipping back to her own eyes, Alex took the reins back from Chine and pointed to a hill in the distance. "Right over there. That's where we're going," she told the other riders.

The dragonriders crested the hill in no time, and all of them stopped at the scene that unfolded before them. There were dozens of dragonriders in the sky fighting bats nearly the size of dragons with no visible riders.

The sky was blood-red, and the clouds were black. Jagged streaks of lightning flashed and thunder boomed. Above the clouds, there was a meteor that looked roughly the size of the Wasp's Nest. Lightning was flying from the meteor, but there was something inside.

Gill wiped his eyes as Jim popped out of his cockpit. "What the hell is that thing?" Gill asked.

Alex pointed at the meteor. "That's where we're going. That's what this whole battle is about."

Jim looked at Alex, confused. "I thought they weren't sending any reinforcements to get Roy and Toppinir?" he asked.

"Sort of. They couldn't afford to send any more reinforcements. Myrddin's been throwing everything he can at this battle. There's just no one else left to go. That's why we're here."

"You really think we're going to change the tide?"

Alex nodded as she gritted her teeth. "It doesn't take much to turn a storm into a hurricane. Come on."

Alex sped upward, and the rest of the team followed her. As they were closing in, Brath said, "Shouldn't we be going over there? That's where the fight is. If they need help, that's where they're going to need it."

Alex doubled down on Chine and sped up. "Not yet. Trust me. We're going to get to the fight. Just not yet. There's something else we have to take care of first. We have to get under it."

"Under the meteor? Are you crazy?"

Alex didn't respond and kept going. They were getting closer. She could smell sulfur in the air from the dragons and bats above. It was impossible to see who was winning, and she had no idea where Toppinir or Roy was, but she knew that meteor was the whole purpose of this mission.

Team Boundless was directly under it. "All right, *now!*" Alex shouted as she ascended, heading straight for the hunk of space rock. She zoomed in between dragons and bats who were fighting, not letting herself lose any speed.

The rest of the dragonriders were right behind her, Jim taking the rear and Gill staying next to him. They fired at any bats that tried to take advantage of Jim's lack of maneuverability.

Team Boundless burst through the last dregs of the battle beneath them, heading straight for the falling meteor.

CHAPTER EIGHT

The meteor was still a couple of hundred feet from Team Boundless, and the battle raging beneath them was trying to fight its way up. Bats had seen the new dragonriders and disengaged to attack Boundless.

Alex did her best to avoid the bats, trying not to get distracted from the meteor. It was difficult, though. The bats were out for blood. Even with her speed, Alex still had to fall back a few times to blast bats who were getting too close.

It didn't look like the bats had riders. They must have been creatures whose only purpose was to serve the Dark One.

At the rear, Jim was taking the most heat from the bats. Luckily, his mech was built for this kind of thing. He deployed his concussive shield, which created a barrier around him so bats hit him and fell away, like birds flying into a window.

Jollies was also doing her best to keep the bats away from the group. She flew, faster than the other dragons, in a circumference surrounding Boundless. As she circled them,

Amber generated electricity, creating a sort of lightning cage to ward off the bats.

Brath flew up to Alex's side. He didn't look happy about what was going on, but Alex could tell the gnome was all in. You only took point if you were ready for whatever was coming.

When Alex had watched through Manny's eyes, she had seen the meteor, but there had been something off about it. Manny's eyes saw different spectrums of light and heat, as well as different planes of existence. There was something in that meteor that didn't fit with the rest of reality.

In Manny's sight, it had looked like flashes of red hot light came off of the meteor but only in one spot. Alex was willing to bet her life on that spot being the meteor's weak point.

This was the same meteor Myrddin had shown Alex when she had first been recruited weeks ago. Alex and her parents had watched this meteor rocketing toward this realm. Myrddin had said it had the potential to turn the tides of the war. He'd said it was the most important campaign at the moment. There had to be a reason Myrddin had shown it to Alex.

Nothing the wizard ever did was without reason. Myrddin had made it a point to show that meteor to Alex. He had made it a point to choose Manny and his eyes to be paired up with this blind girl. And there had to be a reason Chine, with all of his psychic abilities, was bonded to Alex.

Alex raised her hand without thinking. It just felt like the right thing to do. And she slipped back into her mind, focusing on seeing through whatever eyes were within the meteor. She had to know this was more than just a hunch.

A sharp pain wracked Alex's head. She felt nauseous and dizzy, and she stomped her foot down on Chine to make sure she was properly anchored. For a second, she had seen through eyes in the meteor. There was someone in there—

someone who felt familiar. Someone who was waiting for something.

Alex pointed to the lower left quadrant of the meteor and shouted, "Concentrate all your fire on that spot on the left! All of it!"

Brath turned to Alex, his eyes wide with confusion. "Wait, you just want us to shoot at the rock? It's too big! We're not going to be able to make a dent in it. That thing could crush us!"

"Trust me, Brath! Please, just trust me."

Brath stared at Alex as they approached the meteor. His beady eyes were hard to read. Alex couldn't tell if he was thinking about cutting and running or something else. Finally, Brath turned back to the meteor, leaned forward, and went flying straight toward where Alex had been pointing.

Furi let out a tunnel of fire at the left section of the meteor. That fire was followed by Amber releasing lightning bolt after lightning bolt as Jim and Gill finally caught up. Timber fired as well, giant spires of rock flying from her mouth.

Jim hit the back thrusters on his mech and floated, completely stationary, as his mech's missiles locked onto the corner of the meteor. He fired a volley of a dozen warheads that hit the rock, blowing off massive chunks that fell into the battle beneath them.

Chine shot a stream of ether fire as Alex held her breath, hoping she was right. All she knew was that there was something within the meteor.

The smoke began to clear. There was hardly a scratch on the surface of the meteor. *No*, Alex thought.

The dragonriders swooped back, putting more space between themselves and the meteor, which was still descending. "Was that it?" Brath asked. "We didn't even put a dent in it!"

Jollies pointed at the meteor and squeaked, "No! We did! See?"

Alex's eyes hyper-focused on the crust of the meteor. Jollies was right. The surface of the meteor was cracking. "Let's hit it again!" Alex shouted. "This time with everything you got! And I mean everything!"

The dragonriders fired up their various offensive augments. "On my count," Alex said. "One. Two. *Three!*"

The riders blasted out a hailstorm of flames, electricity, gravitational distortion, and missiles. The attacks landed, one after another, breaking into the crust of the meteor. Alex reached out, concentrating as hard as she could. She imagined the crust ripping apart, tearing open to show what was inside.

Alex felt some kind of force extend from her and grip the cracking mantle of the meteor. At first, she thought it was in her head, but then she felt that force grip the meteor hard. The force was coming from her and Chine—from their minds.

Chine and Alex telekinetically dug into the cracking meteor as the rest of the dragonriders continued to unleash hell on it. Alex screamed as her head started to pound, then the left section of the meteor ripped apart, completely separating from the rest.

The chunk of meteor fell through the sky, bursting into flames as if it were entering the atmosphere. Then it stopped falling, floating in the air before the dragonriders as the battle raged below. Intense heat shot out from it.

The dragonriders flew backward, putting more space between them and the piece of meteor. "Uh, was that part of the plan?" Brath asked shakily. "Is the meteor done now?"

Alex ignored Brath and concentrated on what was happening in front of her. Wave after wave of energy was flowing from the chunk. There was definitely something within it. They just had to wait and see what it was.

As if reading Alex's mind, the meteor started to vibrate, shaking violently in the air. It cracked more, flashes of energy sparking beneath the cracks.

The top of the meteor began to bubble. Thick, black slime oozed from an opening hole like some sort of foul afterbirth. A pale hand pushed itself out from the hole, spreading the gap wider as another hand forced itself through.

As the hands touched the air, a black material appeared, wrapping them in shrouds. As more of the pale body forced itself from the meteor, the same material covered the thin, skeletal frame until Holmorth the Dark Wizard of Khaldor stood atop the meteor, his shifting face contorting as if he were only a memory in this reality.

Alex felt her blood boil as she tried to control her breath and stay calm. *He* was what was behind the meteor. It made perfect sense. Only something as evil as he was could want to be responsible for so many deaths.

Holmorth straightened to his full height, reaching down and unsheathing a wispy wand. "Ah, it seems as if we will dance once more," he growled in his raspy voice. "I did not think I would have the chance to kill you all so soon. The gods must be smiling on me."

Brath screamed something unintelligible, and Furi launched a firebolt at Holmorth. The wizard merely waved his wand and the fire disappeared around him. "You're going to have to try much harder than that."

Alex raised her hands and turned to Brath. "Hold on, hold on!" she said. "He's more powerful than he was before. We can't just attack and give him the advantage."

"If he's so powerful, why the hell is he monologuing?"

Alex thought the question through. "You're right. He must

be stalling for some reason," she said. "Dragonriders, get ready to—"

Holmorth raised his wand and bowed slightly. "I am not stalling," he hissed. "Merely playing with my food before the kill. If you are in such a rush to lose your lives, then by all means, let me oblige."

Holmorth floated into the air, his wand raised high. As his feet left the meteor, the crust rapidly deteriorated. Beneath the crust was something foul, reeking of offal and decay, yet encased in what could only be a womb.

The membrane over the embryonic sac was pink and nearly transparent. An eye opened in the fluid, then the membrane burst and the rotting liquid fell to the ground, burning through whatever bat or dragonrider was in its way.

A creature old and horrible uncurled in the sky, its bony tail unwrapping to allow shredded and tattered wings to open. Its body was made of bone, its skin rotting. Maggots poured from its mouth, the undead dragon roaring loudly enough that those who fought below stopped to look up in horror.

Holmorth landed atop the dragon and laughed maniacally. "How does one kill what is already dead?" he taunted. "How does one slay what was born in the very fabric of reality, died, and returned anew, now evil?"

Jim's voice came through on the comm. "That's a really good question. How are we going to kill that thing?"

Alex responded, "I'm glad you're on board with killing it."

Brath was staring down Holmorth and the undead dragon. "Of course, we're going to kill it," he said. "Holmorth killed our friends in cold blood. We don't have a choice. You hardly ever get a chance for revenge. Now we can make him feel every one of their deaths."

Alex had been trying not to think about what had happened at the Wasp's Nest. She didn't want to think of the

dead cadets, their bodies broken and mangled by the inva-
sion Holmorth had led. But Brath was right. Innocent lives
had been lost, children mostly, and it had been Holmorth's
doing.

Alex sized up the dragon as Holmorth stood gloating,
rambling on about a new age of darkness or some other
apocalyptic drivel. The undead dragon was easily twice the
size of Furi. A straight-on fight was going to end up with all
the riders dead. "We go low," Alex suggested. "Back into the
thick of the fight."

Gill chuckled and said, "So, you're opting for running this
time? A bold new strategy."

"Hey, you gotta try something new sometime," Alex said
as she leaned forward, sending Chine diving into the chaos.
The rest of Team Boundless followed closely.

CHAPTER NINE

Team Boundless plunged deep into the battle, weaving between bats and other dragonriders with the undead dragon and Holmorth hot on their tails. Alex knew she was going to have to come up with something better than her current plan.

To be fair, the plan was working fairly well at the moment. The undead dragon was too large to maneuver through the flying bodies. It was more likely to hit a bat than to hit any other dragonriders since the dragonriders were so outnumbered.

As long as Alex could stay out of the undead dragon's way, she would have time to figure out what needed to be done. *Hey, Chine, anything I need to know about undead dragons?*

His answer was hardly encouraging. *Undead dragons are the eldest of all dragons. They are the progenitors of our race, extremely powerful. Even death could not hold them. Their own power brought many of them back to life.*

Okay, but how do we kill it?

The same way you kill any dragon—beat it to death. There is only a little life left in its body. Extinguish the flame that burns within it, and the dragon will remain dead.

Now Alex could see the only flaw in her plan. If the undead dragon was incapable of attacking Team Boundless, the team couldn't go after it that way either. There was too much going on for a straight-on attack. Whatever their next phase was going to be, it would have to be heavy on creativity. "Jollies, you read me?" Alex asked.

The pixie's voice came through the comm crystal-clear. "Yep! You having an easy time dodging all these bats? I swear, I didn't know there were this many bats in the world."

"Not as easy a time as I wanted. I'm going to need you to come with me. We need to start whittling down Holmorth's dragon, and see what Holmorth is capable of as well."

"On it!"

Jollies came zooming through the battle from the other side. Amber and Jollies had speed that Alex couldn't even dream of competing with, and it was that Alex needed at that moment.

Alex and Jollies turned back around, heading toward Holmorth. A group of bats flew at the two dragonriders. They were only able to narrowly pull away at the last minute as the bats sent sonic blasts toward them.

Jollies went low and Alex went high, Alex clearing a path with Chine's ether flames. Once the bats were out of the way, the dragonriders continued toward Holmorth.

Holmorth was waving his wand above his head, lightning crackling from the tip like a whip as he lashed out at the dragonriders around him. He knocked two of them from their dragons and they plunged to the ground, screaming in pain.

Alex noticed lightning seemed to be coming off of the elder dragon's body as well. Maybe Jollies wasn't the best to bring along for this particular plan. "Hey, Jollies, is lightning the only element Amber can use?" Alex asked.

Jollies and Amber buzzed around Chine's head. "No! I got an elemental switcher on her," Jollies answered. "We can go with water, too."

"Hm…water, huh? All right, Jollies, soak the bats directly around the dragon, okay?"

"On it!"

Jollies split away from Alex and started to circle the bats near Holmorth, drenching them in water while Alex occupied herself dodging the lightning attacks Holmorth was directing toward her. "You done yet, Jollies?" Alex shouted.

"Just about! All right, I got them all."

"Good. Now light them up."

Jollies ducked in and out of the bats, Amber's body changing from the softness of liquid to the uncontrollable energy of lightning. A chain of lightning hit the bats surrounding Holmorth, creating a falling lightning cage.

Holmorth raised his wand, waving away the bats that were falling from above. While the wizard was distracted, Alex brought Chine close to the undead dragon's jaw. His claws glowed bright white as he charged.

Chine slashed the undead dragon's jaw, splitting the bone down the middle. The undead dragon recoiled, pulling backward as he unleashed a torrent of ether fire into its face. "Fall back," Alex commanded. "Let's see if we made a dent."

Jollies and Alex backed away from the undead dragon as the rest of her team converged on them.

The undead dragon was roaring in pain—a terrifying noise—but it wasn't going down. In all honesty, Alex hadn't thought it was going to.

Holmorth raised his wand from atop the dragon and aimed it at Team Boundless. All of the bats around him broke off with the dragonriders they were fighting and flew toward

Boundless. "At least we got his attention," Jim said over the comm as he fired his missiles at the bats.

The rest of the riders took evasive maneuvers. Jim had the luxury of being able to tank. He was able to handle an onslaught of bats. All the riders with real dragons had to worry about them getting hurt.

Brath had the most trouble getting out of the way. He struggled to fly through the throngs of bats and dragonriders locked in combat. A bat came at him from the side, ramming into Furi and causing the dragon to spin in the air. Brath grabbed him and held on while the dragon righted himself.

Jollies easily managed to avoid getting hit, but she wasn't in any position to help anyone around her. Gill had broken off with Alex, and the two of them were flying around Holmorth, preparing to flank him.

Holmorth spun to the right as Alex got behind him. He pointed his wand, and there was a flash of red light as a long, slimy tentacle reached out from it. It wrapped around Alex and lifted her in the air.

Alex screamed as she flew through the air, hitting a bat, bouncing off, and freefalling through the sky.

Gill took off after Alex, and as he turned, Holmorth's dragon launched a fireball. It hit Timber in the back, scorching his wings. Timber faltered in the air, twisting, trying to spin to put the flames out.

Alex continued falling, reaching out for something grab, but there were no options. Chine swooped beneath her and Alex fell onto his back. She anchored herself to Chine and caught her breath. *Holy crap! Let's not do that again anytime soon.*

Chine flew back up toward Gill. *The dragon is powerful enough to sever our link. We need to be more careful,* he suggested.

Yeah, I can see that. That thing almost blasted Gill out of the sky with one fireball.

Jim's voice cut through on the comm. "Hey, I got an idea. Wanna give it a shot?"

Alex replied, "Sure, I'm all out of ideas."

"All right. I'm going for it!"

Alex had a faint hint of what Jim was going to try. He knew the limitations of his mech as well as anyone else. He also knew its strengths.

Jim hit his thrusters and went full ahead, aiming at Holmorth. He fired his missiles as he cut a path through the bats in his way. His mech reached out its arms and grabbed the undead dragon's throat, but Jim didn't kill his thrusters. He kept pushing, forcing Holmorth out of the cover of the bats while reducing his dragon's movement.

Alex pitched up and headed toward Jim and Holmorth. "All riders on me!" she shouted as the rest of Boundless raced toward her. "We're surrounding this ass-wipe!"

Boundless surrounded Holmorth as Jim forced the wizard and his dragon completely out of the swarm of bats. The undead dragon was doing its best to get away, and the mech's gears screamed in protest at the dragon's strength.

Jollies went in for the first attack. She aimed at Holmorth, ignoring his dragon. He easily dispelled her first attack, but she had speed on her side. Amber bashed into Holmorth's hand, knocking his wand away.

Next was Gill, swooping in from above as he fired spire after spire of crystals, peppering the undead dragon's back. That was followed by Brath coming from below, Furi spitting fireballs.

Jim pulled away, his mech finally getting near its breaking point. He fired a cluster of missiles as he backed off, blanketing Holmorth in smoke.

Team Boundless waited for the smoke to disappear. Alex

didn't think Holmorth was down for the count yet. She remembered how much damage the wizard had caused in the Wasp's Nest. There was no way he was done.

The smoke settled, and Alex was right. Holmorth and the dragon were still standing, albeit scratched up. The only difference Alex could see was that Holmorth's face looked as if it were starting to settle. Maybe he realized he was in trouble.

Holmorth raised his hands to the sky and screamed as the wind began to whip around, tossing the dragonriders back and forth as a cyclone appeared out of nowhere. As the dragonriders tried to get clear of the twister, Holmorth leaned forward and plunged his hands into the undead dragon.

Bones rose from it and pierced Holmorth through the body, impaling his arms and his chest as he screamed in pain, his face becoming liquid and dripping onto the undead dragon's back.

The wizard and the undead dragon began to fuse, bones popping out of Holmorth's body as his torso grew larger, his legs melting into the undead dragon's until it was impossible to see what was wizard and what was dragon.

Alex and the rest of the riders watched in horror as a dragon's skull burst through Holmorth's head, breathing fire as fireballs floated in the palm of his hands.

Brath laughed nervously and said, "Oh, this looks so much better for us than it did before."

Alex couldn't disagree. Then she heard Chine say, *The wizard has made a dire mistake. He's combined his life force with the undead dragon's. That means you no longer have two enemies, you only have one. Whereas you and I are still two.*

Alex smiled as recklessness made her heart pound. "All right, then I guess it's time to do something stupid. Squad! Keep this freak busy. Time to end this!"

Holmorth roared and shot fire into the sky as he

launched his fireballs at the riders. Alex wove past one, heading for Holmorth. She pulled her scythe from the ether and leaped onto the undead dragon's back, staring at it. "Ready to dance?" she asked.

Chine tackled the undead dragon, grabbing its hands as Jim followed suit, punching its stomach as Jollies flew in and out of the path of its fire.

Brath was flying around the perimeter of the fight, burning through the bats trying to come to their master's aid.

Alex stared at the abomination Holmorth had become. "If you aren't, I am," she said as she slammed her anchor to her chest, unleashing the cataclysm of stored draconian fluid. Her body burst into flames and she sprinted at Holmorth, leaping into the air, her scythe raised.

Holmorth reached out and swiped Alex away, slamming one of the fireballs into her.

Alex skidded across the surface of the undead dragon's back, but the fireball didn't do any damage. Instead, Alex had absorbed it, and her flames were even brighter than before. "Hell, yeah," she shouted as she ran forward.

Holmorth swiped at Alex again, but this time Alex dodged, sliding underneath Holmorth's hand. *Chine! The gravity flux!*

Chine activated his gravity-distorting augments. The effect spread and covered the entire undead dragon.

Alex's feet lifted off its back. She suddenly realized she should have thought that command through; she was floating in the air without gravity. Holmorth, on the other hand, was tethered to his dragon. *One life force*, Alex thought to herself. *And the dragon is barely alive. It's got to be Holmorth.*

Alex reached out and concentrated on the dragon's throat. She envisioned her hand closing around it, choking the life from the creature.

Holmorth stretched his clawed hands toward Alex, who floated like easy prey.

Suddenly, Alex felt the grip. It was not Holmorth's hand around her, but her mind around Holmorth's throat. Alex pulled with everything she had.

Holmorth jerked toward Alex, dropping his fireballs and grabbing his throat. As Holmorth came toward her, she raised her scythe as high as she could. Then she brought it down on Holmorth's head.

The scythe sank into his skull.

"Team Boundless! Unload on this thing!"

Team Boundless released the undead dragon, giving themselves space. Then they fired everything they had without mercy, unloading all of their ammunition into the dragon.

Alex pulled her scythe from Holmorth's skull. The wizard's face started to contort, sloping forward, his teeth falling out, his eyes boiling. He let out a low, pitiful moan.

Alex pressed her hand to Holmorth's head. "This is for the Wasp's Nest," she whispered, focusing her thoughts in one place: the palm of her hand.

The back of Holmorth's head exploded as his body burst into flames.

Alex fell and hit the back of the undead dragon's back hard. All around her, the dragon was coming apart. She ran toward its wings and leaped off, mentally shouting, *Chine!*

Chine swooped down and caught Alex in his paw. Alex climbed his shoulder until she stood on his back.

Alex joined with the rest of the team, who were watching the battle that had taken place adjacent to them. The bats were falling from the sky as if someone had turned them off. "Jim, can you grab one of those?" Alex asked.

Jim flew out and grabbed one of the closest bats in his tractor beam. Gill went over to the bat to get a look at it.

"You won't believe this," Gill said, "but it's inorganic. I think it might be some kind of drone."

Alex didn't even want to think about that bit of information. "Okay, okay. Let's just get on the ground. I think we've earned it."

CHAPTER TEN

Alex and the rest of Team Boundless were the first ones on the ground out of the sky full of dragonriders. As soon as they touched down, Alex said, "All right, let's get these dragons taken care of pronto!"

The riders jumped to it. The process was painful, but didn't take nearly as long as it had the first time. Everyone was able to finish within ten minutes. It was important to Alex to make sure they took care of their companions as soon as possible.

Once the battle had ended, Alex couldn't stop thinking about how much pain Chine must have been in. After seeing the undead dragon and what it had become with Holmorth, Alex realized things had to be different with her and Chine. Always.

He hardly winced during the maintenance, and once Alex was done, he stretched his wings and said, *Thank you. I truly value your attentiveness. The riders above are still congratulating themselves on your victory.*

Alex shrugged, trying not to let the compliment go to her

head. *Don't worry about it. You're important to me. We're bonded. Gotta take care of my boy."*

Brath and Gill were walking over to Alex. "How the hell did you know about that thing?" Brath asked. "You knew exactly where to go and what to do. How?"

Alex laughed at Brath's accusatory tone. "I looked through Manny's eyes earlier. He didn't know what he was looking at, and neither did I, but I knew it was important. So, I guess you both were right. I took another stupid risk."

Gill shook his head as he rested his hand on Alex's shoulder, causing her heart to try to rip out of her chest. "No, I should apologize," he said softly. "I was out of line earlier. You've been doing an amazing job. And that up there...you were like a moving work of art."

Alex stared at Gill, fairly certain she was going to faint. Gill's cheeks turned pitch black, and he started blinking rapidly and cleared his throat as he said, "I meant, force of nature. Like a force of nature."

Brath gave Gill a sideways glance and shook his head. "Uh, I wasn't going to say all that, but it was pretty badass. I mean, really badass."

Jollies and Jim joined the team as the dragons lumbered off on their own. "Couldn't have done it without you guys," Alex exclaimed. "You all were amazing. Can you believe any of that? I mean, Holmorth and the dragon and... I mean, jeez, it's kinda a lot, right? Is it just me? It can't just be me."

Jollies flew over and took a seat on Alex's shoulder. "No, it's not just you," she agreed. "The last few days have been out of control. I could never have imagined I'd fight an undead dragon, let alone blow one to pieces."

Alex gently nudged Jollies' chin. "Well, now you can cross that off your bucket list."

The ground suddenly shook, and Alex spun around to see what was causing the commotion.

A dozen mech riders had just landed. The largest one opened, and Roy jumped out of it. Next to the mech riders, the rest of the dragonriders landed. Toppinir didn't even wait for his dragon to land before leaping off, landing next to Roy.

Roy stormed up to Team Boundless and shouted, "All right, which one of you brats is in charge of all of this?"

All of Team Boundless pointed their fingers at Alex, who, unsurprisingly, was pointing at herself. Roy knelt and got in Alex's face. "What in the nine hells did you think you were doing up there?"

Alex fought against all her inclinations to give a smart answer. She swallowed her pride and remembered why she'd made up her mind to join the battle to begin with. "After we were done with our mission, it came to my attention that you and Toppinir were in a bad situation."

"And?"

"And I disobeyed direct orders to provide you and your squads backup since there were no other dragonriders or mech riders available. Uh, sir."

Toppinir stepped forward and pulled Roy away from Alex. "You do understand that you placed your team in an extremely dangerous position?"

Alex nodded, preparing to say something when Jim spoke up. "Alex didn't put us in any situation. She presented us with a choice, and we all agreed it was the right thing to do."

"And you assumed that neither Myrddin nor the other higher-ups had a backup plan? You assumed you were honestly the last resort?"

"Uh, well, we sort of hacked the system to see what the plan was."

Toppinir's eyes went wide with surprise. "Which one of you broke into our system?" he asked, bewildered and a little impressed.

Gill raised his hand as he lowered his head. "Me. I was watching the correspondence. There was no rescue planned."

Roy and Toppinir exchanged glances. Alex couldn't read their faces. Neither of them spoke until finally, Roy sighed and said, "That's because we weren't expecting backup. Everyone knew the risks when they took this mission."

Alex couldn't keep it in any longer. "But we helped! We took down Holmorth, and now everything's cool!" she interrupted.

"By disobeying a direct order. There's a reason—"

"It was a stupid order! We knew we could help, and we did. I don't see why it's such a big deal!"

Roy and Alex argued, each raising their voice and trying to talk over each other. Toppinir looked as if he had already become bored with the conversation. He had started to gaze skyward. Gill came up to his side and followed his gaze.

The meteor was still hanging in the sky, a green aura surrounding it. "I'm assuming that shouldn't still be there," Gill said softly.

Toppinir looked down at Gill. "There aren't many drow dragonriders," he said unemotionally.

"There is only *one* drow dragonrider. And one human rider, too."

"Hmm." Toppinir nodded, neither impressed nor offended by Gill's directness or tone. "To answer your question, no, that should not still be in the sky. Holmorth was the pilot. We assumed that once he was destroyed, the meteor would be as well."

Gill nodded as he sat down and crossed his legs. "Wouldn't a meteor fall anyway once it's entered the atmosphere?"

Toppinir took a seat beside Gill. "Yes. Yes, it would."

Alex and Roy were still arguing. It was uncertain what it

was about at this point. The tirade hadn't descended into personal insults, but it was getting close.

Jollies squeaked loudly and pointed up at the meteor. "Hey! Do you guys see that? What's going on with it?" Jollies asked.

Alex stared at Roy for a second before turning her attention to the meteor. *Talk about being ungrateful*, Alex thought as she looked up at the meteor. Then any thought of Roy or his opinions quickly vanished from her mind.

The meteor was opening. There was a door where Holmorth had detached from the meteor. The door was slowly creaking open, and what came forth was devastating.

Vrosks, giant bees, and bats came flooding out of the hole in the meteor—more than had been in the sky before. The number had nearly tripled.

Brath jumped on Furi. "You've got to be kidding me," he shouted. "All right, guys, you know what time it is!" He anchored himself and pulled up, causing the dragon to climb to his feet and start flapping his wings.

Alex ran over to Brath, waving her hands to get his attention. "No, Brath, hold on. We need to see what is going on!"

Either Brath didn't hear Alex, or he chose to pretend he didn't. He took off. Roy came up behind Alex, clicking his tongue. "Looks like your squad doesn't care for orders either," he jabbed.

Furi and Brath raced toward the swarm of dark creatures. Something flew in front of him faster than he could see. There was only a blur, and when Brath looked down at his chest, he was bleeding.

Alex focused on Brath and saw him falling from Furi's back. "Brath!" she shouted as she ran toward Chine.

Up above, more creatures poured out of the meteor. There were too many to name, even if Alex had known their names. The sky grew dark as the creatures swarmed, blocking out the sun. The mech and dragonriders stared up at the meteor as the sky went black.

The true danger of the meteor was yet to be known.

The Dark One's deadly meteor is about to land on Middang3ard. But Alex has a plan that just might save everyone. Everyone but her... Find out what it is in *Sacrifices*!

As many of you know, I also write in a universe called the GoneGod World. For the uninitiated, here's the premise:

The gods are gone. All of them. And with their departure, they closed their heavens and hells, exiling their denizens onto Earth. Now mythical creatures of all kinds live among us.

Basically, in the GoneGod World, it is conceivable that Medusa is your neighbor (and depending on where you live, she is!).

Recently I've been writing articles for a fictional magazine in the GoneGod World that, oddly, fit in Middang3ard. In an earlier release, I wrote about the 9 Reasons to Marry an Ogre and They Might Be a Gnome.

In this one I'm exploring Badass Jobs Mythical Creatures are Better at than Humans...

The job market is changing in the GoneGod World, and with an influx of a new and different kind of worker, I'd like to explore six badass jobs that mythical creatures would be better at than their human counterparts.

Now it's easy for this article to digress to the low-hanging fruit ... lazy ideas like a centaur as a carriage driver (they can pull the carriage *and* engage in interesting banter) or a hecatoncheires as a fruit picker (after all, they're giants with a hundred arms).

But such observations are cruel and do not remotely give these amazing creatures their due.

So here are six badass jobs that mythical creatures would be better at than humans:

1 - Deep Sea Explorers: Myraids - or sea-jinni - are the lions of the sea. Fast, strong and vicious, they hunt white sharks bare-handed, can traverse the English Channel in less than eight minutes and can swim to depths that human technology has yet to manage. And with over seventy percent of the world's oceans yet to be chartered, why not use them to help us better understand our world? Who knows what we'll find down there? Other Others? Aliens? Lost civilizations? Resources beyond our imagination? Whatever it is, we can't afford NOT to do it.

Want to see a myraid in action? Azzah appears at the beginning of Keep Evolving (click here:).

2 - Detective: Gorgon

The GoneGod World's favorite gorgon is Medusa, and she's a policewoman in the Keep Evolving Series (click here:).

3 - Houris: Prosecutors

Seleema is the GoneGod World's resident houri, and stars in a short story in the House of the GoneGod Damned (click here:). She'll also star in her own series coming out in 2020.

4 - Enoch's Angels or the Twice Fallen: Archivists

Probably the most famous Twice Fallen is Penemue ... the angel who taught humanity how to read and write. He stars alongside Jean in the Keep Evolving Series.

5 - Dark Elves: Ballet Dancers

I'm just going to say it ... ballet dancers are badass. Their physical prowess rivals a marine, their endurance would put most marathon runners to shame and their muscle control is the envy of Kung-Fu masters. Think I'm exaggerating? Check out Russian Ballet to see the kind of training they go through. But despite all that, they're still just humans and there are limits to what the homo sapien body can do. But a dark elf? Now that's a different story. Dark elves have incredible dexterity, are able to contort their bodies into shapes that no one with a spine should be able to do, treadmills break before dark elves get tired and if a human ballet dancer is as strong as a bull, then a dark elf is as strong as a minotaur.

AUTHOR NOTES MICHAEL ANDERLE
MARCH 5, 2020

THANK YOU for reading our story! We have a few of these planned, but we don't know if we should continue writing and publishing without your input. Options include leaving a review, reaching out on Facebook to let us know, and smoke signals.

Frankly, smoke signals might get misconstrued as low hanging clouds, so you might want to nix that idea.

I have NO idea where Ramy came up with the mythical creatures would be better than humans at <insert job here> concept.

So, just to play along with him, I'll choose firefighter as the occupation. BUT we have a problem (or challenge.) I'm not going to use obviously magical constructs (Ifrit or demon). I'm going to use something...not human.

A Salamander.

But, no *magic*. I'm going to use the mythical quality of the fire salamander that exudes a liquid that provides fire retardant (protective) qualities to whatever it is applied to. Say, the clothes of the firefighters.

So technically, this choice doesn't work better than a

human (still have to save people, pick them up, etc.) but rather, in a symbiotic relationship, those firefighters who have fire salamanders as collaborators will be able to deal with horrible fires better. Their equipment will have a special *mythical* you might say protection against the dangers of the heat and flames that others do not.

Ad Aeternitatem!

Michael Anderle

OTHER BOOKS BY THE AUTHORS

Other Middang3ard Books

Never Split The Party (01)
Late To the Party (02)
It's My Party (03)
Blue Hell And Alien Fire (04)

Death Of An Author: A Middang3ard Novella

Other Books by Ramy Vance

Mortality Bites Series
Keep Evolving Series
Fatebound Series
Welcome to the Dragon Show Series

Other Books by Michael Anderle

For a complete list of books by Michael Anderle, please visit:

www.lmbpn.com/ma-books/

All LMBPN Audiobooks are Available at Audible.com and iTunes. To see all LMBPN audiobooks, including those written by Michael Anderle please visit:

www.lmbpn.com/audible

CONNECT WITH THE AUTHORS

Connect with Ramy

Join Ramy's Newsletter

Join Ramy's FB Group: House of the GoneGod Damned!

Connect with Michael Anderle and sign up for his email list here:

Website: http://lmbpn.com

Email List: http://lmbpn.com/email/

Facebook:
www.facebook.com/TheKurtherianGambitBooks

www.ingramcontent.com/pod-product-compliance
Lightning Source LLC
Chambersburg PA
CBHW050157110726
47898CB00008B/2833